Did you know that the colours in this book are made from vegetable-based inks?

EGMONT
We bring stories to life

First published in Great Britain 2020 by Egmont UK Limited
2 Minster Court, London EC3R 7BB
www.egmont.co.uk
Text copyright © Smriti Prasadam-Halls 2020
Illustrations copyright © Ella Okstad 2020
Smriti Prasadam-Halls and Ella Okstad have asserted their moral rights.

ISBN 978 1 4052 9566 6
Printed in Italy
70616/001

A CIP catalogue record for this title is available from the British Library.

For ingenious Rafi – king of the kitchen – who is resourceful, big-hearted . . . and ALWAYS has a plan. S.P-H. xx

For my kids: HC, PA, OJ and our cat L. E.O.

Elephant
in my Kitchen!

Smriti Halls
Ella Okstad

EGMONT

There's an elephant in my kitchen,
It's true, I KID YOU NOT!
She's found the chocolate biscuits . . .
She's eating up the lot!

When I asked politely
Who had let her in,
She lifted up her great big trunk . . .

A gorilla's in my bedroom.
He's pulling out my toys!
He's made the most ENORMOUS MESS
And loads and loads of NOISE.

A rhino's reading stories,
While BOUNCING on the BED.

A panda's playing BADMINTON
With KNICKERS on his HEAD.

A tiger's on the toilet
And I'm BURSTING for the loo!
He says it's just a number one . . .

It's definitely a TWO!

An orangutan is brushing,
There's TOOTHPASTE in his EAR,
Would someone kindly tell me please . . .
What ARE they doing HERE?

A polar bear is in the freezer . . .
EATING OUR ICE CREAM!
She's licking all my lollies.
It makes me want to scream!

A penguin's pecking popcorn,
A wolf is wolfing cake,
A chimpanzee is mixing up
Banana-chocolate shake!

It's HOURS past my bedtime
But the frogs have started CROAKING.
I cannot stand much more of this
And I'm not even joking . . .

So when they found Pink Rabbit,
And when they squashed him flat,
I shouted, "Oi! I've had enough of this!
IT'S TIME WE HAD A CHAT!"

So . . .

Oh dear. . .

It turns out that . . .

There's hardly any fish to eat,
And hardly any ice.
Their homes are disappearing,
Well, THAT'S not very nice!

The trees keep getting chopped away.
There's RUBBISH in their bed.
There's barely any food . . .
And so they're round MY HOUSE instead!

It's our fault!
WE'VE GOT TO DO SOMETHING!
Because . . .

Tigers live in forests
And NOT on our settee.

Whales should NOT take bubble baths.
They should be in sea!

Elephants drink water,
NOT my fizzy pop.

Snow leopards need the mountain tops . . .

THIS HAS GOT TO STOP!

We'll make their houses cosy.
We'll make them safe and strong.

We'll give them peace and quiet
To live where they belong.

Our world belongs to everyone,
Let's make sure that we share . . .

Let's work to save our planet
And show them that we care.

Because if we cannot
change our ways
And fix our world
together . . .

The animals will have to come and live with me . . .

FOREVER!

THE BIG PLAN

WE LIVE HERE!

EARTH

HOME →

PROTECT THE PLANET AND **ALL** OUR FRIENDS ON IT!

PICK UP LITTER!

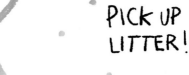

SWAP– DON'T THROW AWAY!

NO MORE PLASTIC STRAWS

WALK AND CYCLE MORE!